majikkids
presents...

The Master's Apprentice

Bradley T. Morris and Sauryn Majik
Illustrated by Albert K. Strasser

ISBN: 978-1-7778939-1-0 (Paperback)
ISBN: 978-1-7778939-0-3 (Hardcover)

The characters in this book are entirely fictional. Any resemblance to actual persons living or dead is entirely coincidental. Names, characters, and places are products of the author's imagination.

Written By: Bradley T. Morris
Illustrated By: Albert K. Strasser
Book Design By: Sarah Van Alstyne
Edited By: Amy De Nat

Printed by IngramSpark, Inc., in the United States of America.
First printing edition 2021
IngramSpark
14 Ingram Blvd,
La Vergne, TN
37086,
United States

www.MajikKids.com

I dedicate this story to my son (Sauryn), my wife (Celeste) and to all of the young masters-in-the-making around the world. My hopes are that this story inspires you to stick with the things you enjoy doing most so that someday you have the joy of achieving mastery in them.

-Bradley

I dedicate this story to Mommy, Papa, Amma and to my good friend Daeus.

-Sauryn

For my mom, who believed I could draw before I did

-Albert

A long, long time ago,
Not far from the beach,
Lived a wizard named Gizzard
Whose turn it was to teach.

2

He waited and waited
For someone he could show,
But he couldn't find anyone
Who was ready to learn and grow.

Magic
Lessons

3

MARCH

So, he waited...

JULY

and waited...

TICK TOCK

SEPTEMBER

And he waited some more,

Until his beard grew so long it nearly touched the floor!

4

But as he waited, he practiced
And mastered every spell.
Yet, still there was no one
To show, teach, or tell.

While he practiced,
His beard grew quite long and fat,
Until he had to tie it in spirals
Up in his hat.

Then, finally came the day
When a lad entered his shop,
And he asked lots of questions.
He sure did ask a lot!

And suddenly, old Gizzard—
Like a lightbulb switching on—
Realized this young lad was whom
He'd been waiting for all along.

He waited for the lad to stop
And finally catch his breath,
And then the wizard asked,
"Would you like to walk
the wizard's path?"

The young lad stuttered, "Yes!"
And his excitement said it all.
And just like that, old Gizzard
Had a student he could call.

His apprentice was named Lentice.
He was a passionate little kid.
He loved learning about magic,
And did everything Gizzard did.

But Gizzard was much better,
For he'd practiced many years,
Which filled Lentice with frustration,
And he'd sometimes break down in tears

He'd stomp and throw his wand away,
Yelling, "I'll never be as good as you!"
Gizzard just responded,
"In time, you'll do more than I can do."

So, Lentice, breathing deeply,
Would wipe his angry tears
And get back to his learning.
He did this for many years.

As Lentice grew much older,
His temper could be worse.
He'd forget a spell or something
And feel like he would just burst.

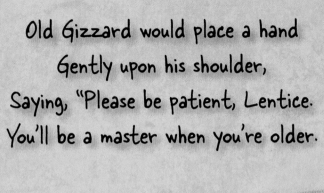

Old Gizzard would place a hand
Gently upon his shoulder,
Saying, "Please be patient, Lentice.
You'll be a master when you're older.

Just practice every day
And you will go from good to great."
But Lentice would reply,
"I want it now; I don't want to have to wait!"

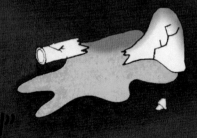

The old wizard would just smile, with a twinkle in his eye,
Which helped Lentice to remember his big, important reason WHY.

He didn't do it cause he had to; it was because he truly loved it. He loved magic more than anything, and he never would forget it.

16

...and for the final touch...

17

From that day on, young Lentice
Enjoyed magic more than ever before.
Even when he made mistakes,
It was a chance to learn and explore.

For many years he practiced.
He practiced day and night.
He rose at dawn each morning,
Before the sun shone down its light.

THIS, he thought, is the thing
that I was born to do.
And he did it every day,
as his mind and body grew.

Over time he learned all Gizzard's tricks
And taught him a few of his own.
Eventually, the long-bearded wizard
Had showed Lentice all he had ever known.

Happy with his apprentice,
The wizard knew his end was near,
So he called him to his office.
He had something for Lentice to hear.

"You've been a dedicated student.
You've been a joy for me to teach.
I've passed to you my wisdom.
You've reached beyond where I could reach.

I just hope that you remember
Why you do what you choose to do.
It's not for accolades or status,
Or that you have anything to prove.

It's for the love of making magic,
And the way it makes you feel.
As long as you stay true to that
Your joy for it will stay real.

24

I have brought you here today
To thank you for all these years."
As Lentice listened, Gizzard could tell
He was trying to fight off tears.

"But, Gizzard, I'm not ready.
I need you by my side."
"Worry not, young Lentice.
I'm just going fishing at high tide.

If you need me, I will always be
In your heart—or just over there—
So get back to work, because I'm retired
And have nothing left to share."

And then, with the wave of his wand,

Gizzard said, "Alakafloat."

And just like that — *POOF* —
He appeared out in his boat.

For years and years
Lentice continued to practice every spell.
Eventually, he'd mastered all of them,
And it was now his turn to tell.

- EXCUSE ME MR. WIZARD!
I HAVE A FEW QUESTIONS!

So, like Gizzard the wizard,
Lentice waited for a student to appear.
And, one day a young girl showed up,
And her excitement made it clear.

The next apprentice was born,
And Lentice would teach all he knew.
And eventually, she would surpass him
And do more than he could do.

and the beginning

Join the **majik**kids club !

Be the first to hear our new stories & meditations, access our downloadable colouring books, get games, activities, cool conversation starters, discounts on books and other magical stuff that's fun for the whole family! Enjoy a sample of what's included in the Majik Kids Club in the following pages...

Visit us at majikkids.com !

Conversation Starters

Either answer the questions in writing inside the lined area OR better yet, share your answers with a friend, at the dinner table with your family or with your class. This is a fun way to get to know the people you love spending time with.

If you could be a master at anything what would it be?

_____

_____

_____

_____

_____

_____

What are some things you could do everyday that would help you become better and better at that thing?

_____

_____

_____

_____

_____

_____

In the blank box below, draw a picture of your 30 year old self being a Master at that thing.

To listen to an audio version of this story
and to find many more magical books,
join the Majik Kids Club at majikkids.com!

 **Bradley T. Morris** is the creator of
Majik Kids, founder of Majik Media. He loves writing
stories, making cool media and waking people up to
remembering that life is truly awesome and magical. His
passion-hobby is playing pro golf.

 **Sauryn Majik** is the co-founder of Majik Kids.
He's also five years old. He also loves making up stories,
laughing, playing and using his imagination to create
worlds. He also thinks adults need to have more fun and
lighten up a bit.

 **Albert Strasser**, author of the hit kids
book, *Afraid of the Light*, is a pacific northwest based
writer and illustrator. A devoted student of life, Albert loves
creating stories that inspire, empower, and uplift children
and grownups alike. He hopes you enjoy them as much
as he enjoyed making them.